Albe's Apple

by Tara Seiden Furgiuele

Illustrated by Elizabeth Uhlig

Marble House Editions

Published by Marble House Editions
96-09 66th Avenue (Suite 1D)
Rego Park, NY 11374
dougeliz@worldnet.att.net
www.marble-house-editions.com

Library of Congress Cataloguing-in-Publication Data
Furgiuele, Tara Seiden
Albe's Apple/by Tara Seiden Furgiuele

Summary: A young boy living out in the country steals a prize apple from a neighbor's tree and finds a way to redeem himself.

ISBN 978-0-9815345-4-1
Library of Congress Catalog Card Number 2009923533

Printed in China

To my biggest fan

Once upon a time, way out in the country, there lived a boy named Albe.

Albe liked to help on the farm, play catch with his dog Buster, and pull his red wagon along the country roads.

Whatever it was that Albe was doing...

4

...he could never resist an apple.

He liked all kinds of apples. In fact, there was no type of apple that Albe did not like.

Red Delicious

Granny Smith

Golden Delicious

Pink Lady

And Albe liked anything made of apples.

Candied Apples

Apple Cider

...and especially

Apple Pie

One day while Albe was out exploring, he came across Mrs. Johnson's apple orchard where a huge apple tree stood. Albe could not believe his eyes.
There before him was the most perfectly shaped, beautifully shiny apple.

I'll bet it tastes as good as it looks, thought Albe, his mouth watering.

9

Albe knew the apple did not belong to him and that he should just keep walking. Instead though, he started to think of reasons why he *should* eat the apple.

Apples are **supposed** to be eaten!

It would be such a shame for this apple not to be eaten!

An apple a day keeps the doctor away!

With that, Albe simply could not resist. He plucked that apple right off Mrs. Johnson's tree and took a great big bite. Just as he thought, it was the crispiest, juiciest, sweetest apple he had ever tasted!

When Albe finished the apple, he smacked his lips and went on his way.

13

The next week, Albe passed by the Johnson orchard again. As he was remembering the apple he had enjoyed there, he spotted Mrs. Johnson sitting under her tree. She was crying.

"Why Mrs. Johnson," Albe said, "what's the matter?"

"Oh, Albe," Mrs. Johnson sobbed, "I am sad because I won't be able to compete in the countywide Grandest Apple Contest! My prize apple is missing from the tree!"

Albe started to feel cold all over. "Well, um....maybe you can enter the contest with one of your other apples."

16

"These are fine apples, Albe, but they are the same ones that you can buy at the farmer's market. I don't think this old tree will ever grow another apple quite like that one," she sighed.

"Back when I was a little girl, this tree was full of prize-winning apples, but over the years, there have been fewer and fewer of them."

Albe could not stand it any longer. "Oh, Mrs. Johnson," he blurted out,
"I ate your prize apple. I am so sorry!"

"Albe, Sweetheart," Mrs. Johnson replied, "you know that if you want something that doesn't belong to you, you should ask permission before you take it. I would have been happy to give you that apple *after* the contest."

"Mrs. Johnson, I am so sorry. I promise never again to do something I know is wrong."

"I think you learned a valuable lesson, Albe. You are a good boy and I accept your apology."

20

All during the next week, Albe could not free his mind of the picture of Mrs. Johnson crying. He tried working on the farm, playing with Buster, and pulling his wagon along the country roads. But none of these made things any better. He just felt terrible about what he had done.

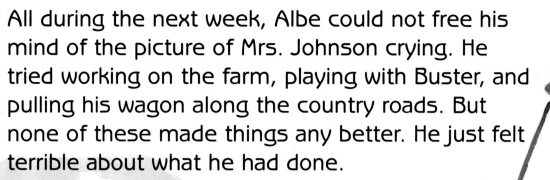

Then Albe found a solution. He decided to shower Mrs. Johnson's apple tree with love, in the hope that it would grow another perfect apple.

All winter,

…all spring,

...and all summer, he attended to the tree with great care. He watered it, raked up the dead blossoms that fell, and made sure the birds that nested in it were safe.

Then one day that fall, as Albe was passing the Johnson orchard, he saw something unbelievable. There before him stood Mrs. Johnson's tree, covered with glorious apples, one nicer than the next!

Albe ran to Mrs. Johnson's door with the news. "Mrs, Johnson, Mrs. Johnson, it's a miracle!" he shouted.

The old woman smiled, for she had already seen all the splendid apples. "It is not purely a miracle, Albe. My tree is vibrant once again because of the way you cared for it."

That year, Mrs. Johnson won the blue ribbon in the annual Grandest Apple Contest.

28

As they left the fair that day, Mrs. Johnson turned to Albe and said, "Albe, I know it was your tender loving care that brought my tree back to life, and so I would like you to pick all the apples you want from my orchard."

"Well, Mrs. Johnson," Albe replied, "what I would really like is *this* winning apple so that I can take the seeds and plant my very own apple tree."

"Surely you may have this apple," Mrs Johnson said. "Now, what shall we do with all the other apples on the tree?"

"I know!" Albe said. "Let's invite everyone in the county back to your orchard so that we can enjoy them together.

A smile crept across Mrs. Johnson's face. "That is a great idea, Albe. You certainly are a good boy."

Later that fall, people from all around came to taste the wonderful apples
from Mrs. Johnson's tree. And as long as Albe kept on showering the tree with love,
it produced the shiniest, crispiest, tastiest apples in the county.

31